Wendy's Big Game

based on a book by
Diane Redmond

with thanks to
HOT Animation

SIMON SPOTLIGHT
New York   London   Toronto   Sydney   Singapore

Based upon the television series *Bob the Builder*™ created by HIT Entertainment PLC
and Keith Chapman, with thanks to HOT Animation, as seen on Nick Jr.®

SIMON SPOTLIGHT
An imprint of Simon & Schuster Children's Publishing Division
1230 Avenue of the Americas
New York, New York 10020

Manufactured in the United States of America

First Edition

2 4 6 8 10 9 7 5 3 1

ISBN 0-689-85460-9

One morning Bob had some news for the team. "Hello, everyone!" he said.
've entered us in the Brightest Building Yard competition, and we have to
ean up before the judges arrive."

"When are they coming?" asked Roley.

"Five o'clock," Bob replied.

"You'd better get started then," said Wendy. "Muck can help you, Bob.
The rest of the machines can come with me. We've got to get the soccer
field ready."

"**Can we do it?**" Wendy yelled as they roared out of the yard.

"**Yes, we can!**" cried the machines.

When Wendy and the machines got to the field, Scoop began to unload
the cans of white paint. Wendy filled up the line-marking machine.

"I need to get this grass as flat as I can," said Roley. "If I leave any bumps,
the ball will bounce all over the place."

Wendy marked out a goal line. Scoop unloaded the wood for the goalposts, and Roley flattened the ground. But Dizzy was bored and wanted to play soccer.

Suddenly Spud jumped out from behind a bush. "I'll play with you!" he said.

Dizzy passed the ball to Spud, who gave it a huge kick! The ball flew high into the air, then dropped slowly down.

"Oh, no!" squeaked Dizzy. "It's going to land on Wendy!"

Wendy looked up just in time and saw the ball heading straight at her. Dragging the line-marking machine, Wendy ducked sideways. The ball missed her by only a few inches!

"Where did that come from?" she asked.

"Uh, Wendy," said Scoop, "look what you've done."

Wendy gasped when she saw the wiggly line she'd made on the field. "Sorry, Wendy," said Spud. "I was just showing Dizzy a few soccer tricks." "Well, now you can get a bucket and brush and show Dizzy a few cleaning-up tricks," Wendy said.

Back at the house, Bob was busy clearing the yard. He had swept up huge pile of garbage—and Pilchard found it! She curled up on a warm, sunn spot on top of the pile and was soon fast asleep.

Muck came roaring back into the yard with a front dumper full of plants and flowers. "Here I am, Bob!" cried Muck.

"Well done, Muck," said Bob. "Let's unload those plants. Then you can clear away that pile of garbage."

While Bob arranged his flowerpots, Muck scooped up the garbage in th
back dumper.

"Me-ow!" cried Pilchard.

Bob turned around. "Oh, no! Muck, stop!" he yelled. "You've scooped up Pilchard with the garbage!"

Muck slammed on the brakes, and garbage went flying all over the yard. "Sorry, Pilchard," said Muck. "I didn't know you were up there."

Bob brought Pilchard down safely.

While Bob was hanging a flower basket, Bird settled into it.
"Tweet!" he chirped happily.
"Bird, I know my pots make a lovely nest, but you're squishing my flowers," said Bob.

Bird flew off, but Bob found him a few minutes later on top of another plant.

"You're squishing those flowers too, Bird," Bob said, sighing. "I don't think I'll ever have the yard clean and ready by five o'clock!"

Meanwhile, Wendy and the team were almost done with the soccer field. Lofty had lifted the goalposts into place. Roley had flattened the field perfectly. Scoop had helped Wendy build the bleachers, and Spud had even cleaned up the wiggly white line.

"Oh, Wendy," Dizzy squeaked. "Can we please play a game?"
Wendy checked her watch. "Well, we've got time. We don't have to be back at the yard until five."
"Yippee!" cried Dizzy as she raced down the field after the ball.

Wendy blew the whistle to start the game. Dizzy kicked off. And when
Lofty got the ball, Dizzy jumped in and sent it up the field to Spud. Spud
trapped the ball and headed it over to Wendy. Wendy dribbled the ball
toward the goal—and kicked it in!

"Goal!" yelled Dizzy. "Hooray for Wendy!"

"Oh, that was fun!" said Wendy. "But we must get back to the yard. It's almost five."

Bob's yard was finished in time too. It looked very neat and clean, but Bob was covered in dirt! "I'd better clean up before the judges arrive," he told Muck.

Just then they heard a car driving up. "Oh, no," said Bob. "The judges are ere early!"

Wendy and the machines came back to the yard and were surprised to see how clean and neat it looked. "Bob did a great job," said Wendy.

Suddenly Bird landed on one of the flowerpots. "Bird, get out of there before the judges arrive," Wendy said.

"It's too late," Bob said. "The judges have already come and gone."

"Really?" asked Wendy. "What did they say?"

Bob held up an award. "We won!" he exclaimed. "Our yard won first prize in the Brightest Building Yard competition!"

The machines cheered. "Whoo-hoo! Yippee!"

"Oh, Bob, that's wonderful," said Wendy. "Well done!"

"The yard looks clean, Bob," said Dizzy, "but you're all dirty."

"Lucky for you it wasn't the Brightest *Builder* competition," said Wendy, laughin

"You're right about that, Wendy!" Bob s